C480011700

D0314749

WITHDRAWN
NEWCASTLE UPON
CITY LIBRARIES

Newcastle
City Council

Newcastle Libraries and Information Service

☎ **0191 277 4100**

Due for return	Due for return	Due for return
. . . .	. . . .	. . . .
. . . .	. . . .	. . . .
. . . .	. . . .	. . . .
. . . .	. . . .	. . . .
. . . .	. . . .	. . . .
. . . .	. . . .	. . . .
. . . .	. . . .	. . . .
. . . .	. . . .	. . . .
. . . .	. . . .	. . . .
. . . .	. . . .	. . . .
. . . .	. . . .	. . . .

Please return this item to any of Newcastle's Libraries by the last date
shown above. If not requested by another customer the loan can be
renewed, you can do this by phone, post or in person.
Charges may be made for late returns.

Illustrated by Vince Reid

First Published
October 09 in Great Britain by

NEWCASTLE U, ON TY
CITY LIBRARIES

Class No.	Acc. No
JF	C 4801
Checked	Issue ⊙
	1/18

PUBLISHING

© Adam Bushnell 2009

All rights reserved. No part of this publication may be reproduced in any form or by any means without the written permission of the publisher.

The moral right of the author has been asserted in accordance with the Copyright, Designs and Patents Act 1988

A CIP record for this work is available from the British Library

ISBN-10: 1-905637-85-3
ISBN-13: 978-1-905637-85-0

Typeset by Educational Printing Services Limited

Educational Printing Services Limited
Unit 6, Glenfield Park 2, Northrop Avenue, Blackburn BB1 5QH
Telephone: (01254) 686500   Fax: (01254) 686501
Email: enquiries@eprint.co.uk   Website: www.eprint.co.uk

Contents

King Frodi

A very long time ago the sea didn't contain one grain of salt. It was full of beautiful and clean water. You could place a cup into it, scoop out some water and drink it down in one gulp. And it would still be that way today if it wasn't for greedy King Frodi.

King Frodi was a wealthy and powerful king. He lived in a large palace on a large island in the middle of the sea.

***

One day, a one-eyed old man came to visit King Frodi.

"I have sailed from afar to your island, King Frodi. I have brought you gifts!"

King Frodi looked at the one-eyed stranger with suspicion but said, "You are welcome as a guest in my palace."

The stranger was given food and

1

shelter. His boat was looked after by the harbour master.

After a few days of living in the palace as the King's guest the stranger announced, "King Frodi you are a good and kind king. For your warm hospitality, I give you a gift. I give you magic millstones. If you turn them, they will grind for you *anything* you want. For now, I bid you a fond farewell."

The one-eyed stranger then had the harbour master and his workers take the magic millstones from the stranger's boat and put them into King Frodi's throne room.

With that, the stranger set sail across the water and disappeared forever.

King Frodi looked at the magic millstones. They looked like any other millstones – just two large, heavy, circular stones.

The King grabbed the wooden handle in the centre of the two stones and tried to turn them. But they were stuck fast.

King Frodi's servants then tried; but they couldn't make them move either.

Nobody could make the magic millstones turn.

King Frodi and his servants tried many

more times, but not one person on the island could make them turn, not even a millimetre.

The King often said, "If only somebody could make these magic millstones turn! I would make my people so happy! I would grant them all that they could ever want!"

**

One day, two golden haired women arrived at the palace.

"We have been told that King Frodi is a good and kind king. We are here to find out . . . We are here to make your magic millstones turn."

King Frodi greeted them warmly and said, "You are welcome in my palace!"

He took them to the throne room where the magic millstones were kept. The two women took hold of the wooden handle of the magic millstones and said, "What shall we grind for you?"

"I would like peace and happiness for all my people," smiled King Frodi, "and some gold too, so that none of them will go poor."

The two women began to turn the magic millstones and as they did they began to chant, "Grind . . . Grind . . . Grind . . .

Grind out peace and happiness for King
Frodi's people and gold too. Grind . . . Grind .
. . Grind."

Peace and happiness swept the whole
of the island, but when King Frodi saw those
golden coins pouring onto the ground his eyes
got wider. He rubbed his hands together and

said, "I think my people need more gold . . . grind some more!"

The two women turned the magic millstones and chanted, "Grind . . . Grind . . . Grind . . . Grind out gold for King Frodi. Grind . . . Grind . . . Grind."

The gold poured out all over the floor of the room and as it did, King Frodi's eyes got even wider. He rubbed his hands together even more quickly, "Keep grinding!" he cried, "I want enough gold to fill this whole room . . . NO! . . . I want enough gold to fill this whole palace . . . NO! . . . I want enough gold to fill this whole island! Keep grinding!"

After a while the two golden-haired women began to slow down.

"Why are you slowing down?!" shouted King Frodi.

"We are tired," the two women replied, "we need to rest."

"You can rest for as long as it takes to say King Frodi . . . King Frodi! There, you've had your rest, now start grinding again!"

The two women looked at each other and said, "King Frodi is no longer a good king. We should stop him."

They smiled and as they turned the

magic millstones they chanted, "Grind . . .
Grind . . . Grind . . . Grind out fierce warriors
to kill King Frodi. Grind . . . Grind . . . Grind."

As they turned the millstones ten fierce
warriors appeared in the room.

All wearing shining armour. All
carrying swords and shields.

Twenty of them.

Thirty of them.

They made a large circle around King
Frodi.

They pointed their swords towards him
and began to walk forward. The circle got
smaller and smaller as they got closer and
closer until,

"AAAAAAAARRRRRRGGGGGGGHH!"

King Frodi collapsed dead on the floor.

***

But here were thirty fierce warriors in a land
that had just been given peace and happiness,
what would they do here?

The fiercest of the warriors said, "We
shall steal a ship from the harbour, we shall
steal the magic millstones and kidnap the
golden-haired women and set sail across the

sea. We shall kill. We shall make war with every island we come across!"

And so the fierce warriors stole a ship from the harbour and set sail with the magic millstones and the golden-haired women on board.

When they were in the middle of the sea the fiercest of the warriors turned to the women and said, "You! Golden-haired women! Show me how these magic millstones work, grind something for me!"

"What shall we grind for you?" they asked.

"Grind anything. Salt if you must. Just show me how these magic millstones work!"

The two women began to turn the magic millstones and as they did they chanted, "Grind . . . Grind . . . Grind . . . Grind out salt for the fierce warriors . . . Grind . . . Grind . . . Grind."

Salt poured out onto the deck of the ship.

It got deeper and deeper and deeper.

The fiercest of the warriors said, "Stop grinding! You'll sink the ship!"

But the two golden-haired women didn't stop, they said, "Grind . . . Grind . . . Grind . . .

Grind out salt for the fierce warriors and never stop grinding!"

The ship sank to the bottom of the sea taking with it the fierce warriors, the golden-haired women and the magic millstones.

Those magic millstones are there today. Still grinding. And that is why, from that day forward, the sea is salty.

The Wyrm, the Eagle and the Beetle

Askelad sat by his father's side. He knew that the old man was dying but wanted to make his passing as comfortable as he could. Askelad bathed his father's brow, gave him sips of water from the stream and told him stories.

Before the old man died he gave his only son the only thing he had to give. His sword and kind words, "Askelad, I give you my sword. I ask you to always be honest and listen to your heart."

With those words said, the old man died.

Askelad wept.

He then picked up the rusted, brittle sword, packed some bread and set off to find his way in the world.

As he walked he heard a terrible commotion coming from over the other side of a rocky hill. Askelad climbed to the top.

Looking down he saw a huge legless dragon . . . a wyrm!

The wyrm was shouting, bellowing and arguing; Askeland couldn't see who it was arguing with. Suddenly it stopped. It turned its head and looked directly at Askelad.

"OI, YOU!" it bellowed, "GET DOWN HERE AND HELP US!"

"Erm, me?" whimpered Askelad as he skidded down the other side of the hill towards the ferocious scaly beast.

"YEAH, YOU!" it boomed, "YOU CAN HELP US! MY FRIENDS AND I NEED YOU TO HELP SETTLE AN ARGUMENT!"

Askelad saw that the wyrm was with two animals; a great eagle and a tiny beetle. The three unlikely companions stood over a dead horse.

"WE NEED YOU TO HELP US DECIDE WHO WILL EAT WHAT!" thundered the dragon.

"Yes," began the eagle, "which part of this horse will be eaten by my friends and which will be eaten by me?"

"Divide it up with that sword!" squeaked the beetle.

Askelad scratched his head and set to

work slicing and chopping up the horse. When he had finished, Askelad noticed that the rusty old sword had broken in two. He felt sad for breaking his father's sword but decided not to mention it and instead said, "How about these big joints of meat for the wyrm? He is the largest of you all and needs the most food!

"Then the liver, legs and fiddly bits for the eagle? He should get the best as he's such a fussy eater!

"Finally the head should go to the beetle! He would like to creep and crawl inside the skull for his dinner, I'm sure!"

The three companions smiled and nodded, then began their feast.

They talked to Askelad for the rest of the day; telling their stories and songs.

"DID YOU SNAP THAT SWORD WHEN YOU DIVIDED UP OUR DINNER?" bellowed the wyrm.

"Indeed I did, my friend," said Askelad sadly, "but no matter."

"THAT'S NO GOOD!" boomed the wyrm. "WE OWE YOU. I DO KNOW A BIT OF MAGIC AND I THINK I CAN GIVE YOU A VERY USEFUL GIFT!"

Suddenly the wyrm let out a blast of hot, steamy breath over Askelad. It shocked the boy at first, but it didn't hurt him. He felt warm and tingled all over.

"What did you do?" he asked.

"I'VE GIVEN YOU THE POWER OF TRANSFORMATION!" thundered the dragon, "NOW YOU WILL BE ABLE TO TURN YOURSELF INTO ANY ONE OF US WHENEVER YOU LIKE. JUST THINK OF BEING A WYRM; AND YOU WILL BE. SAME IF YOU WANT TO BE AN EAGLE, OR A BEETLE. ENJOY!"

With that the three companions set off, thanking Askelad for his help and his companionship.

Askelad climbed back up to the top of the hill.

He closed his eyes and imagined himself as an eagle.

And he was!

Askelad the eagle soared into the air and flew above the hills and mountains for many miles.

Eventually, he grew tired, so landed in a tree next to a large palace. Suddenly he was grabbed and stuffed into a golden cage.

The Princess of the palace had seen
Askelad the eagle land and thought he would
make a beautiful pet. She took him to her
bedroom and placed him on a table. She then
rushed off to the kitchen to get some cuts of
meat to feed to her new bird.

Askelad imagined himself as a beetle.
And he was!

Askelad the beetle then walked out of
the cage and turned back into a boy.

When the Princess returned she was

astonished.

"Who are you? What are you doing in my bedroom? Where's my new pet?!" she demanded.

"My name is Askelad!" beamed the boy.

"GET OUT!" she screamed.

Askelad climbed onto the windowsill, imagined himself as an eagle and flew off.

As he was leaving, a huge giant came stomping across the land. Askelad the eagle landed in that same tree again and watched what would happen next.

The King's guards emerged from the palace shooting arrows and waving swords, but they were all swept aside by the monstrous giant.

It punched a hole through the palace wall, reached inside, grabbed the Princess and set off with her. His massive fingers encircled her entirely, but Askelad could still hear her screaming.

The King ran out of the palace calling after his daughter but eventually sank down to his knees and wept in despair. Askelad imagined himself as a boy and leapt down from the tree.

"Don't worry!" he said, "I'll save your

daughter!"

The King looked at the boy through his tears and simply shook his head. Askelad became an eagle and flew off in pursuit of the giant and the Princess.

It was easy to follow such a big thing. Each step the giant took made a thundering, booming noise until it arrived at a gigantic cave. It stepped into the darkness then rolled a huge boulder across the entrance to stop anyone else from entering.

Askelad the eagle landed on the ground, imagined himself a beetle then crawled in through a tiny gap.

Once inside, Askelad the beetle saw the giant build a fire and set a large cauldron over the top filled with water. He then looked at the Princess in his massive hand and smiled a toothy, drooling grin.

Askelad the beetle imagined himself as a wyrm and roared with fury.

The giant was so surprised that he dropped the Princess, but Askelad the wyrm caught her with his tail and set her gently down.

The giant landed a punch on Askelad the wyrm's head and he was knocked to the other side of the cave.

A ferocious battle then followed.

The giant punched, kicked, butted, bit

and scratched.

Askelad the wyrm ducked, weaved, rolled, coiled and uncoiled until he saw his chance. With his long teeth he lunged and ripped out the giant's throat. Blood sprayed the walls of the cave and the giant fell down dead.

Askelad the wyrm then used his mighty strength to push aside the boulder blocking the exit. He then imagined himself as a boy and turned to face the Princess.

Hand in hand they walked back to her palace. It had only taken Askelad the eagle a few moments to fly the great distance from the palace to the giant's cave; but the walk back was much longer, especially as the Princess and Askelad the boy took their time. They enjoyed each other's company, and fell in love along the way.

When they arrived at the palace, the wedding preparations began. In no time they were married. Askelad the boy became Askelad the Prince and eventually became Askelad the King.

Family of Evil

Weyland the blacksmith was having a fitful dream. It had been seven years since his beautiful wife, Hervor, had been transformed into a swan and flown away. He dreamt of her every night. Where could she be?

Weyland sat up with a start. Had he imagined that noise coming from his blacksmith's shop?

Probably not. Weyland was the greatest blacksmith the world had ever seen. His work was like none other. He had seven hundred golden rings in his shop, each one as beautiful as the first. It wouldn't have been the first time someone had tried to steal them.

Grabbing his sword, Weyland jumped from his bed and ran next door to the shop.

Thirteen soldiers, wearing chainmail and helmets, carrying swords and axes, were filling a large sack with all seven hundred of the golden rings.

Weyland roared with fury; sword-drawn he attacked them. But he was overpowered, disarmed and bundled into another large sack.

The journey seemed to last forever.

Eventually the blacksmith was dumped from the sack onto a luxurious rug in a throne room.

Weyland adjusted his eyes to the light and saw a king on his throne.

He had a bushy, black beard and eerie,

emerald eyes. The King frowned menacingly, casting a shadow right across the worn face.

"You may rise, Blacksmith," barked the King.

Weyland stood up. He recognised that face and he gulped. He stood in front of King Nidud. Nidud the Nasty. That's what everyone called him behind his back. You would never say it to his face as Nidud the Nasty's favourite hobby was torturing people. He had a dungeon deep below the palace filled with tools for torture.

He had a wife and three children, two boys and a girl, who were meant to be as nasty as Nidud.

The King was holding one of the golden rings to a candle and smiled as it twinkled in the light.

"Nice work, Blacksmith," said King Nidud with a sinister grin on his face.

"It's mine," Weyland said boldly, "give it back to me."

The King stood up, shaking with fury, then suddenly seemed calmer. "Bring me my dagger," he barked.

Servants hustled and bustled and bowed. One of them handed King Nidud a jewel encrusted golden dagger with a blade as long as a dragon's tooth. The Queen squealed with delight and the two sons began to laugh loudly.

"Hold him."

Servants leapt upon Weyland and had him pinned to the ground in an instant.

"Hold his legs."

Weyland struggled but knew it was of no use.

"You will be my servant. You will be my blacksmith. You will make me beautiful objects. You are mine."

"Never!" shouted Weyland in defiance.

King Nidud smiled. "You will be taken to a desert island and left there. My servants will visit you once a day. If you have made gifts for me then you will be rewarded with food and drink. If you have not, then you will starve. To make sure you do not try and escape, I will leave my mark upon you."

King Nidud brought the blade to rest behind Weyland's knee. He smiled and sliced the tendons of both legs and laughed deeply. The King's wife and sons laughed too.

Weyland screamed and was dropped to the floor.

"You have been hamstrung*. You will never walk again."

The servants then wrapped Weyland in the luxurious rug and took him to a rowing boat.

Weyland found himself on a small rocky island surrounded by choppy waves. There was a small house and a blacksmith's shop built specially for him.

Weyland crawled to the house, to the bedroom, to the bed and slept. When he awoke the pain was immense. He sat on the side of the bed, stood up and managed to walk a few steps, but that was all. Looking at the wound, Weyland didn't think the tendons had been completely cut. He thought that perhaps he would walk again; eventually.

He would need food and drink to recover. To heal.

The blacksmith sighed and struggled to the shop to begin his work.

Every day King Nidud's servants would

* The hamstrings are the tendons at the back of the knee that link them to the thigh. To be hamstrung means to have the hamstrings cut.

collect the gold, silver and bronze creations that Weyland had made. In return they left him food and drink along with the gold, silver and bronze for the next day's work.

But Weyland had a plan. An escape plan. He could not walk far, but perhaps he would not need to.

The blacksmith had begun to collect a little of the gold, silver and bronze left for him. He crafted three feathers each day. A gold feather, a silver feather and a bronze feather. Each one paper thin.

After many days, Weyland's wings began to take shape. If he could not *walk* off the island then perhaps he could *fly* away, as his beautiful wife had done seven years ago.

One day, King Nidud's daughter arrived on a little rowing boat.

"Hello," she said timidly, "I'm the King's daughter."

"What do you want?" asked Weyland suspiciously.

"I hate my father. I hate my whole family. They are cruel. Evil! I want to help you."

"Why would you want to help me?" Weyland still eyed the girl suspiciously.

"I love you." The Princess sighed, "I have loved you since the moment I first saw you. I hid in the throne room and heard you stand up to my father. I have loved you ever since. What can I do to help?"

"If you do love me then I am sorry," said Weyland, "for my heart belongs only to my wife and I must find her. But if you wish to help me, then send your two brothers to me tomorrow. I have gifts for them. Now leave me."

The Princess burst into tears and rowed away from the island, slowly, sadly.

But Weyland smiled. His escape was now complete.

He worked like a demon all that day and night.

The next morning a boat arrived with King Nidud's two sons on board.

"Well?" one of them demanded. "Where are our presents then?"

Weyland held out a golden sword with silver patterns swirling all around.

"I'm having that!"

"No you aren't! It's mine!"

The two brothers rushed towards Weyland and the blacksmith brought the sword crashing down. He chopped off their heads and began to work once more.

When the servants arrived the next day, Weyland heard them gossiping about the missing princes. The King and Queen were frantic with worry. Weyland smiled and handed the servants the King's latest gifts and accepted the food, drink, gold, silver and bronze.

That night, Weyland's wings were ready. He spread them wide and took to the sky.

He flew to King Nidud's palace.

He flew to King Nidud's bedroom window.

He flew to King Nidud's bedside.

"Rise King Nidud!" bellowed Weyland.

The King and Queen leapt from their beds.

Weyland menacingly held out the golden sword he had made. With the gold, silver and bronze wings, he looked like an angel of death!

"Did you like my last gift to you?" asked the blacksmith while pointing at the golden, jewel-encrusted goblets on the bedside tables.

"Y – y – yes," stammered the King.

Weyland smiled and said, "I made them from the skulls of your two sons. I used their eyes for the jewels. I used their teeth for decoration. You are a family of evil and you will never see me again!"

Weyland stepped to the windowsill and flew into the night sky, listening to the cries of torment and misery from King Nidud and his wife.

The blacksmith simply kept flying . . . searching for his long lost wife.

And that was the last that was ever seen of him.

The Sea Troll

There was once a fisherman called Thorstein. He went out in his little fishing boat every morning and sold whatever he'd caught at the market place during the afternoon.

He had three daughters and a wife to look after so he didn't mind his work one bit. They worked hard looking after him so he worked hard looking after them.

But one day, while Thorstein was rowing his boat over some mighty large waves underneath fearsome-looking clouds, a great green hand emerged from the sea and grabbed the boat.

"Help!" shouted Thorstein. "The Sea Troll's got hold of my boat!"

But there was no-one to listen.

The green hand pulled and tugged at the boat. Thorstein was thrown this way and that.

Suddenly, the Sea Troll peered into the

boat. He was a horrifying sight; two bulging eyes sticking out from green, slimy skin. A long, crooked nose poked out for what seemed forever. His hair hung like black seaweed all about the place and his teeth looked like broken glass when he smiled.

"Helloooooo," the Sea Troll boomed, grinning. "Have you any daughters then, eh?"

"Y – y – yes," stammered Thorstein.

"Oooooh, yummy!" beamed the Sea Troll, "I do love fishermen's daughters! I'll let you go but I'll be round for one tonight! Ta-ra!"

With that, the Sea Troll disappeared under the murky waves.

A stunned Thorstein rowed his boat back to the shore. He then glumly plodded his way to his home.

"You're back early," smiled his wife, Astrid.

Thorstein didn't say anything. He sat on the sofa and began to cry.

His daughters gathered around him; Haldana, Hulda and little Helga.

"I – I – I'm sorry, I'm just so sorry," wept Thorstein.

He then explained all to his family.

"Perhaps he won't come!" said Haldana.

"Perhaps he'll forget!" agreed Hulda.

There was only silence in the house for the rest of the day.

But that night there came a terrible banging at the door.

Thorstein opened it and there stood the Sea Troll.

He stuck his huge face into the house and said, "Helloooooo. Who is comin' with me then, eh?"

The family stood, stunned.

The Sea Troll then grabbed Haldana, ran off to the beach and swam away.

The next day, Thorstein couldn't go fishing. Astrid couldn't do her work, Hulda and Helga just held each other, sobbing.

And so it remained all that day until night fell. Then there was another terrible banging at the door.

Thorstein opened it and there stood the Sea Troll again. He stuck his huge face into the house and said, "Helloooooo. That one was no good, so who's comin' with me next then, eh?"

The family stood, stunned, sorrowful.

The Sea Troll grabbed Hulda and swam

off again.

The next day, Thorstein, Astrid and Helga wept the whole day long.

And so it remained until night fell. Then there was *another* terrible banging at the door.

Thorstein opened it and the Sea Troll stuck his huge face into the house and said, "Helloooooo. That one was no good either, so you're comin' with me!"

The Sea Troll grabbed Helga and went off to the beach. They splashed into the water and the Sea Troll took Helga deep down to the seabed. He pushed a rock at the base of the cliff, and swam up into the passage until they arrived into a deep, damp, dark cave.

There, Helga saw her two sisters sat, shivering and cold, on a rock jutting out of the water.

"Helloooooo you two. I've got your sister!" laughed the Sea Troll. "Will you marry me pretty little one?"

Helga looked at her sisters, thought for a moment and said, "Yes."

"Helloooooo, my wife to be!" bellowed the Sea Troll and began to splash about the cave with excitement. "Give us a kiss then!"

Helga closed her eyes, gulped and kissed the Sea Troll on his long, crooked nose.

The Sea Troll gave Helga warm clothes and blankets, fine wine and food, gold and silver presents. When he wasn't looking, Helga slipped her two sisters a couple of blankets, food and drink.

The next day, the Sea Troll went off to gather food for the wedding and brought back a whole herd of cows.

"We won't need that many!" laughed Helga. "Send one of those cows in a sack to my parents' house as a gift. They'll be your family soon too!"

The Sea Troll grumbled and groaned but did as he was told. When he wasn't looking, Helga beckoned her sisters to climb into the sack too and hide underneath the cow.

When the Sea Troll picked up the sack he said, "Helloooooo. This is a heavy cow, I'll tell you that!"

"Don't be such a baby!" laughed Helga. "You're big and strong, aren't you?"

The Sea Troll puffed out his chest and set off to Thorstein and Astrid's house.

The wedding day soon arrived. The

Sea Troll told Helga to tidy up the cave and cook the cows while he went and fetched the wedding guests. Helga tidied, dusted and cleaned; she cooked all but one of the cows over the fire.

When the feast was laid out on the table, Helga dressed the cow in a fine wedding dress, placing a veil over the face for disguise. She then sat the cow facing the fire and hid behind a large rock.

When the Sea Troll came home he said, "Helloooooo wife-to-be. Meet the lads!"

Helga could see gigantic trolls of all shapes gathering in the cave. Some were hairy, others were scaly, some were warty, others were spotty, but all were ugly!

"Hellooooo wife-to-be. I said meet my mates!"

But the cow in the wedding dress sat stock still.

The Sea Troll was getting impatient, "Helloooooo wife-to-be. Answer me!!"

The Sea Troll lost his temper and pushed his cow bride, who fell into the fire. The wedding dress went up in flames and the cow burnt to ashes.

"You great idiot!" called one of the trolls.

"You've killed her!" shouted another.

"It wasn't his fault!" came a reply.

"She wouldn't answer him!"

"That's no reason to kill her!"

"Yes it is!"

"No it's not!"

There was a great raging argument for a while; trolls began pushing each other this way and that way. Fists began to fly. Clubs began to swing. Rocks were thrown. Skulls were smashed.

Eventually every one of the trolls was wiped out. All dead. Even the Sea Troll himself.

When all was done, Helga crept out from behind her rock and as she was about to leave she noticed a huge amount of gold stacked up in the corner of the cave.

She filled a sack with gold, climbed down to the bottom of the cave, swam back to the rock at the entrance, pushed it open and swam to shore.

When she returned home her family were overjoyed. They were reunited and had so much gold that none of them ever had to work again.

Prince Sigurd and
the Dragon Fafnir

Odin was the King of the gods and lived in
the clouds in a city called Asgard with all of
the other gods. He only had one eye as the
other one had been plucked out and dropped
into Mimir's well. This sacrifice had made
Odin all-knowing. He understood the way of
the world and how it was all balanced and
entwined. He understood the language of the
birds. He knew everything.

Odin had many children but his
favourite was his son, Thor, who was a brave
and powerful warrior.

The one-eyed god wanted children on
Earth too. So he made Sigurd. A Prince on
Earth.

But Odin did not have time to raise the
boy; he was a god and was needed in Asgard.

So he commanded that the dwarf
blacksmith, Regin, be the guardian of Sigurd

and that he raise the boy as his own.

But Regin was jealous of this boy prince.

"Why should he be getting all of this attention? He doesn't do anything. All he does is strut about telling everyone he's the son of Odin. So what? He's no hero.

"And I'll show everyone . . . I'll show everyone on Earth that this boy is weak and puny!"

***

One day Regin woke Sigurd early, "Morning sleepyhead!" smiled Regin. "Time to get up; you've got a big day ahead of you, so you'd better practice!"

"Ey . . . what? Why . . . what are we doing?" asked a sleepy Sigurd.

"I'm your guardian here on Earth. It's my responsibility to make sure you live up to your title of Prince," Regin began. "It's time you had your first quest. It's time you started acting like a son of Odin. It's time to slay a dragon!"

Sigurd sat up straight. "A dragon?!"

"The dragon Fafnir!" beamed Regin. "But first you'll need a sword. I'll get to work straight away and make your first sword ever!"

Regin went straight to his blacksmith's workshop and Sigurd could hear him hammering away. The noise was deafening but not as deafening as the hammering of Sigurd's own heart in his chest. Nervously, he dressed and arrived in the blacksmith's shop to see Regin holding a very hastily made sword out to him.

"It's very light, isn't it?"Sigurd said as he slashed with the sword this way and that.

"All part of my skill," grinned Regin.

Sigurd then brought the sword crashing down onto the anvil to test its strength and the sword shattered into a hundred pieces.

"Look what you've done now!" shouted Regin.

"Sorry," blushed Sigurd.

Regin got to work and again made a very flimsy sword in no time at all. Sigurd began to swing the sword this way and that then brought it crashing down on the anvil. This sword shattered as easily as the first and Regin howled with fury, "Why do you keep doing that?! Of course it will break if you smash an anvil with it!!!"

"But dragon skin is meant to be tougher to pierce than an anvil!" replied Sigurd, "I only want to be sure I'm prepared."

Regin grumbled and made a third sword and presented this wobbly weapon to Sigurd.

Sigurd took the sword and said, "Thanks Regin. Can we go dragon hunting tomorrow? I need to pray to my father and ask for his guidance."

"I suppose so . . ." mumbled Regin and sneaked off into town to buy some ale.

While he was gone, Sigurd tested this third sword on the anvil and again it shattered after just one strike. He didn't want to tell Regin and hurt his guardian's feelings, so Sigurd gathered all of the pieces of the three swords and crafted his own, thicker, stronger sword.

Sigurd struck the anvil which split into two. The Prince then held the sword aloft and said, "I shall call you Gram, for you will be my wrath!"

Sigurd then said a prayer to his father, asking for guidance and strength.

The next morning Sigurd and Regin were up before dawn and the two set off to the dragon Fafnir's cave.

They hid among the rocks and watched as the giant creature slithered out of the dark entrance, stomped a few paces then took flight looking for its breakfast.

"He's very big, isn't he?" gulped Sigurd.

"It'll be easy," smiled Regin. "Just dig a pit near the entrance to the cave; climb in and hide. When the dragon comes home he'll walk over the top of you. That's when you open up its belly with that fine sword I made you. The belly is the softest part of the dragon!"

"Great idea!" beamed Sigurd and leapt down to the entrance to Fafnir's cave.

He began digging as fast as he could and in no time was sitting in a large hole waiting, sword in hand, for the dragon to return.

Just then an old man peered into the hole. Sigurd saw that the old man had only one eye.

"Hello there young man," smiled the old man. "What are you doing?"

Sigurd explained all and the smile faded from the old man's face.

"But if you open Fafnir's belly, his blood will pour into your hole. Dragon's blood is like fire; you'll be burnt alive! Tell you what. Why don't you dig another hole? Right next to this one. That way, after you've opened up the dragon's belly you'll be able to roll into the other hole and be safe from the boiling, burning blood."

The old man smiled and then disappeared.

Sigurd peered out of his hole but the old man was nowhere to be seen.

The Prince shrugged and did as he was

advised. He dug a second hole and hid back in the first.

Just then, Fafnir came home.

As the huge dragon stomped over the top of the hole, Sigurd plunged his sword, Gram, into the scaly belly. He then leapt into the second hole as the dragon roared with anger and collapsed onto the floor, dead. Fafnir's blood poured into the first hole and filled it up to the top. Sigurd leapt from his hole screaming and shouting and cheering.

But Regin arrived looking very put out.

"You did it then?" he asked glumly.

"YES!!!" beamed Sigurd. "Yes, I did!"

Regin kicked a stone along the floor then smiled, "You have done well. So well that we should celebrate. Cut out Fafnir's heart. Cook it over an open fire. I shall eat the heart in your honour and your name. We'll then travel into town and I'll tell everyone what you have done here today. How's that sound?"

"Fine," smiled Sigurd, "you get the fire going and I'll cut out the heart."

Regin busied himself making the fire and preparing the frying pan.

Sigurd used Gram to cut out Fafnir's heart once all of the blood had poured out of the dragon.

"Ale!" cried Regin, "I need ale with my feast! You cook the heart and I'll get us a few bottles, eh?"

Sigurd smiled and nodded as Regin skipped off to get the ale.

As the heart cooked over the fire the Prince stirred it round and round. Some of the juices from the heart splashed onto Sigurd's hand, so he licked them off.

As he did, he felt a wave of warmth spread all over his body. He suddenly saw a small bird fly past. It was a wren. A wren with just one eye. It sat on Sigurd's shoulder and whispered in his ear.

"The juices from this heart have made you understand the language of the birds. Imagine what would happen if you ate the whole heart."

Sigurd nodded and immediately began devouring the dragon's heart. As he gulped down the last mouthful, Sigurd became all-knowing. He understood the way of the world and how it was all balanced and entwined. He not only understood the language of the birds, he knew everything. He knew that Regin had been trying to trick him all along. As his

guardian returned, carrying the ale, Sigurd
drew Gram and chopped off Regin's head.
It rolled into the hole filled with Fafnir's blood
and dissolved into nothing.

Sigurd felt ready. Ready to be a warrior.
Ready to be a Prince. Ready to be Odin's son
on Earth.

The Death of Balder

Odin, the King of the Gods and Frigga, the Queen of the Gods, were delighted. Twins! They had twin boys. Delighted as they were, they did notice how very different the boys were.

The first, they named Balder. He was bright, beautiful Balder. A child of light and beauty.

The second was Hoder. He was dark, deep Hoder. A child born blind.

The proud parents loved their two boys very much. Balder became the God of Light and Hoder the God of Darkness. They were opposites but got along very well.

Eventually Balder fell in love and married the young goddess Nanna. They were very happy and lived in a silver and gold palace. Asgard, the city of the gods, was a much brighter place with Balder in it. Even blind Hoder felt it was.

But Loki, the God of Fire and Mischief was not happy. Loki the trickster, Loki the shape shifter. Loki hated Balder, and he sent him nightmares. He unleashed the Marra, a demon that delivers nightmares. Terrible dreams to torment Balder. Dreams of his own death.

Odin noticed the change. His shining son was paler than before.

"What is the matter my most beloved son?" asked the worried Odin.

"Nothing Father," Balder flashed a dazzling smile. "It's nothing, please don't worry."

But Odin persisted and Balder told him of the terrible nightmares. Odin hugged his son and told him not to worry.

Frigga was distressed when Odin told her of Balder's terrible dreams. She fretted as a mother frets about her beautiful son.

So Frigga decided to do something. She travelled all over Asgard, then down to Earth. She spoke to every living thing and the things that did not live. She spoke to the whole of creation and made everyone and *everything* promise not to harm Balder.

Earth promised, the gods promised,

trees, animals, fire, water, air, metal, disease, sickness, poison . . . all of creation in this world and every other promised that they would not harm Balder.

Frigga returned, exhausted, to Asgard. She called all of the gods for a meeting. "Nothing will harm Balder now," she beamed.

There was a huge celebration. Balder felt much better, much *brighter* straight away. The gods rejoiced and the party commenced.

Only Loki was unhappy. He sulked and plotted as the gods played.

They invented a new game. They took Balder to a meadow in Asgard and threw things at him. Rocks, sticks, spears, swords, axes all bounced off Balder. Nothing could harm him.

What a new game this was! The gods were having a great time. Loki used the opportunity to slip away. He transformed himself, and became an old woman. He hobbled to Frigga's palace where the Queen was resting after her long quest.

"Pardon me, Your Majesty," croaked the old woman, "but to celebrate the joyous news I have brought you a gift. Seven golden apples for you and your husband to enjoy."

Frigga thanked the strange old woman and smiled. She was pleased that everyone delighted in Balder's health.

"Is it true that nothing can harm the dear boy?" crooned the old woman.

"No nothing," replied Frigga.

"Nothing at all? Are you sure?"

"Well," answered Frigga, "there is just *one* thing. It's so small though. I didn't speak to the mistletoe. It is such a small weedy thing that grows on trees. It doesn't even have its own roots; it has to rely on the strength of the tree. But that could not possibly harm him anyway!"

"Of course, it couldn't!" laughed the old woman before bidding the Queen farewell.

Loki changed himself back to his

normal sly form. He was grinning from ear to ear. The trickster rushed to the tree near the gates of Asgard and pulled down the mistletoe plant growing on it. He used a knife to sharpen a twig into a dart. Then he used his magic to make it hard as a rock.

Loki joined the other gods in the meadow and they were still hard at their game. They were being more imaginative with what they threw at Balder. Chickens, geese, even pigs; everything bounced off him. The God of Light took it all with a smile, delighted he was making others happy. But Hoder looked glum. He stood by the side of the meadow listening to the fun his brother and his friends were having and he couldn't join in.

Loki crept up next to the God of Darkness.

"You could join in if you wanted," soothed Loki, "I could help you aim."

"Why would you do that?" asked Hoder suspiciously.

"You just look so sad and everyone else is so happy," Loki replied in smooth tones. "Here, take this dart and throw it at your brother. I will guide your arm."

So Loki placed the hardened mistletoe dart in Hoder's hand. He helped him take aim and Hoder threw. The dart pierced Balder's chest. The light slipped from his face and he fell down dead in an instant.

Loki had slipped away before Hoder knew what had happened. Frigga was sent for. Odin thundered with sadness and rage. Nanna wept. Hoder despaired. The gods were bewildered.

"Who will go to the Underworld?" Frigga suddenly asked. "Who will travel to the Kingdom of the Dead and speak to Hel, Queen of the Dead? Who will beg for the safe return of Balder?"

"I will go!" boomed Odin.

"No, dear King! Let me go!" Hermod, Messenger of the Gods said, "I am the fastest here. Let me go!"

"Then take my eight legged horse! He will make you even faster!" Odin replied as he rushed to get his magical horse.

In a flash Hermod was away, out of Asgard, below the Earth and into the Kingdom of the Dead. There he found Hel, Queen of the Dead, and begged for Balder's return to life.

"You claim that all things love Balder," said Hel, "then prove it. If all things weep for Balder . . . if creation cries for the death of the shining one . . . then I will let him go."

Hermod smiled. He turned the horse back away from Hel and sped off. He rode faster than light out of the Underworld, past the Earth and back into Asgard where he delivered Hel's promise.

A great cheer went up in Asgard.

And creation wept for Balder.

The gods wept, the humans wept, animals, plants, even giants wept for the death of light and beauty. The birds wept, the grass, the trees, even stones wept for Balder.

But Hel would not release him.

She sent a raven with a message for the gods, "One creature will not cry for Balder. One being withholds tears."

Odin sent all of the gods across the whole of creation to find out who would not grieve for the death of his son. Eventually, Hermod found the creature; an evil giantess refused to weep.

Odin saddled his magical horse and went off to find the evil giant woman. When he did, the King of the Gods saw that it was

Loki in disguise. The trickster turned himself into a salmon and plunged into icy water to escape the wrath of Odin. But Odin caught him and dragged him back to Asgard.

There, Odin chained Loki to sharp rocks in a deep cave. Above his head, Odin bound the most poisonous snake in all of creation. The poison dripped down onto Loki and burned him.

And there Loki still remains. Waiting for the rebirth of this world and every other. Only then will he be free from his torture.

But then Balder will be reborn as well. And all of creation will have its light and beauty back.

Beowulf

Once there lived a great king. His kingdom knew only victories and greatness. But death comes to us all. The great King met his doom in a battle with terrible beasts of darkness.

The kingdom fell apart. Brother fought against brother. Sickness and famine spread everywhere. Until only one remained. He could see nothing but death before him, so he gathered all of the kingdom's treasure and hid it in a cave, deep in the earth.

This last man stood on the barrow* above the cave and instructed the earth to keep safe the golden pile until the once great kingdom was rebuilt.

These were his last words.

***

Many winters passed. The land remained

*Barrow: mound of earth and stones usually placed over a grave.

stark and lifeless.

Until there came a flying, scaly monster. A wyrm. A dragon. This beast had ravaged the lands of the south and came north to find a resting place. The gold filled cave was just the place. The slick skinned creature oozed its way underground and curled up on top of the mighty pile.

There, it slept. It slept in the darkness. It slept and waited . . .

***

Thousands of winters passed. The lands of

the south had prospered. Another great king had risen. King Hrothgar ruled the land of the Danes. To celebrate this prosperity and peace, a Great Mead Hall was built. Hrothgar named it Heorot and it was glorious. No hall was like it anywhere else in these lands. It was taller than the tallest of trees and wider than the widest of rivers.

Heorot was not just a place for the wealthy. Everyone in Denmark was invited to a feast to celebrate its completion. The Danes danced and sang and drank and made merry.

But, the noise of this celebratory feast woke something. Something that lived in the land of Cain, the land of marsh and forest. Grendel the demon awoke from his rest. He could not bear the sound of cheering and shouting. He held his great claws over his ears and bellowed in fury.

Then Grendel tore across the land and burst open the doors of Heorot. He roared his terrible roar and the Danes were frozen with fear. Grendel was monstrous; he was covered in hard, bony scales which no weapon could pierce. He had razor sharp claws and teeth. His eyes burnt with a demon-like fury, searching the hall for the Danes within it.

The warriors of Heorot leapt into action and hacked at Grendel. But their weapons were useless.

Thirty warriors were ripped apart in seconds, their blood flowing like a red river through Heorot.

Then, as abrupt as his arrival, Grendel returned back to the land of Cain.

Heorot, and its people, were devastated. Hrothgar wept at his loss.

Each night Grendel returned to Heorot and anyone in the Great Hall was torn apart.

Many heroes challenged Grendel. And many heroes died.

Heorot stood empty. There was a curfew in Denmark. Everyone had to stay indoors at night as this time belonged to Grendel.

***

Twelve long winters passed. News of Hrothgar's trouble travelled to the north. In Geatland, King Hygelac's warrior, Beowulf, heard of Grendel.

Beowulf stood before his King and spoke, "My King. My friend. I wish to travel to Denmark and beat this beast Grendel. Our brother Hrothgar needs our help. Do you wish me to go?"

King Hygelac consulted the stars and prayed to God. Beowulf was given fourteen of the best Geat warriors and a mighty ship built from the wood of the rowan tree to protect him.

They sailed through giant waves and ravaging storms until they landed on the shore at Denmark.

The fifteen warriors leapt onto the beach and were met by a coastguard. The Danish guard challenged Beowulf and his warriors and asked them why they had come. Why they wore chain mail. Why they carried weapons of war.

"We have heard of your trouble," said Beowulf, "we are here to defeat the dreaded Grendel. Take us to Hrothgar and all will be well."

The coastguard led the fifteen Geat warriors to Hrothgar's home and vowed to look after the rowan tree ship until they returned.

Hrothgar had heard of Beowulf's reputation. Of his famed strength of thirty men. The warriors were welcomed in the land of the Danes. Beowulf turned to his men gathered before him and spoke, "I am Beowulf. I who have battled the Blood Beast. Clashed with the Troll Clan. Slain nine sea serpents. I will kill Grendel this very night."

A huge roar went up and Hrothgar ordered mead and food to be brought to Heorot. Once more the Great Hall would know the sound of celebration.

Only Unferth, Hrothgar's cousin, challenged Beowulf. He asked why he thought that he would be successful when so many others had failed.

Silence reigned in Heorot. All eyes were on Beowulf as he replied, "I will defeat Grendel. But I will not need my mail or sword. I will use my hands to defeat the demon."

Then Beowulf threw his sword and chain mail to the ground before Unferth.

Another great roar went up and the celebrations continued.

Darkness crept across the land and the mood changed in Heorot. The Danes began to creep off to their beds leaving the fifteen men from Geatland to guard Heorot.

Beowulf and his warriors climbed under covers and faked sleep as they waited.

They did not wait long. The doors
of Heorot were opened and in stepped the
gigantic Grendel.

He sniffed the air around and let out a
moan of joy as he could taste the sweet smell
of human blood in the air.

Grendel crept through the hall sniffing
and tasting the air with his serpent like
tongue. Then with an insect like ferocity,
Grendel grabbed one of
Beowulf's
warriors from
under his
covers and
bit deeply.

The warrior screamed a death moan and the other fourteen men leapt into action. With blood on his teeth, Grendel roared his terrible roar and attacked. The warriors hacked at Grendel but no weapon could get through his hard and bony scales. The demon then lashed out knocking thirteen men across the hall, where they fell unconscious.

Beowulf was the only warrior left. He grabbed Grendel and with his mighty strength they began to wrestle with each other. They wrestled this way and that across the whole of Heorot.

But Grendel soon began to realise his error. He knew that his strength was no match for Beowulf's. He tried to retreat and headed for the door. But Beowulf's grip held fast. He grabbed the monsters arm even tighter and pulled Grendel back away from his exit.

To and fro they went across Heorot. Back and forth. Until, a last, tendons began to split. Bones began to burst.

With an ear splitting roar Grendel's arm was ripped off. He screamed and ran out of Heorot and back to the land of Cain.

There, he staggered down to the beach

and fell into the murky sea, dead.

Back in Heorot, Hrothgar and the Danes appeared and another huge celebration was held.

Grendel's arm was nailed to the wall and the Great Hall of Heorot was repaired.

The Danes danced and sang and drank, then sat in silence and listened to Beowulf's story.

Then Unferth stepped forward and begged for Beowulf's forgiveness for doubting him. Unferth then gave Beowulf his sword, as a gift.

Hrothgar lavished many gifts upon Beowulf. The Geat warrior was given a banner embroidered with golden thread. A chain mail shirt, sword and helmet also made from gold. And eight horses with golden saddles.

"These lavish gifts are more than generous," said Beowulf, "I will give these to my king, Hygelac. And to you King Hrothgar, I give Heorot. Your mead hall is safe once more."

Hrothgar wept with gratitude and gave Beowulf and his warriors homes of their own on Danish soil.

Hrothgar and the Danes then slept peacefully in Heorot . . . but not for long.

***

When Grendel died, his blood flowed into the sea and drifted down to an underwater cave. There, the Sea Hag, Grendel's mother, tasted her son's blood in the water. Swift as a seal, she swam to the shore and saw her son's bloody body lifeless on the beach.

She howled with fury and grief. Then stomped her way through marshland and forest to Heorot.

She silently pushed open the doors and stepped inside. The Danes slept all around her. The Sea Hag then unleashed her claws on Aeshere, Hrothgar's advisor. She wrapped her talons over his mouth and dragged Aeshere outside without a sound.

In the morning Hrothgar noticed his friend's absence and sent for Beowulf and his warriors. The King told them of his fears that there may be a second beast in Denmark and begged that they accompany him on a search for Aeshere.

"If there is another demon in Denmark,

then fear not Hrothgar. Beowulf is your guardian and champion. Vengeance is better than grief. Let us make ready for our search and pray to God that Aeshere is safe from harm."

Beowulf then donned his golden chain mail and carrying his sword at his side, mounted one of the horses with the golden saddle.

Hrothgar and Beowulf led the Dane and the Geat warriors on the trail of green blood that Grendel had left behind to the land of Cain. There, they walked past twisted trees and bushes in frost bitten woods. The horses' hooves crunched the frozen heather below. Eventually they passed a haunted lake and reached the seashore.

Aeshere's head was all that remained of him. Hrothgar let out a howl of sorrow.

Beowulf leapt from his horse, muttered a silent prayer and leapt into the water.

Serpents wriggled around Beowulf's body as he dived further into the depths, but they made no attack.

Down, down, down went Beowulf.

From deep below, the Sea Hag raced and grabbed the warrior with her monstrous claws. She dragged him to her cave under the sea. This enchanted cave was filled with air rather than water and gave the Geat the chance to fill his lungs rapidly. The Sea Hag threw Beowulf across the cave and onto jagged rocks.

Beowulf drew his sword and leapt into action. He landed a mighty blow on the Sea Hag's neck. But the sword shattered into a hundred pieces on her hard and bony scales.

Taking out a curved dagger, she knocked Beowulf to the ground, leapt upon him and began to hack at his body with the blade. The golden chain mail Hrothgar had given him held fast though, and Beowulf pushed the witch away from him. Glancing around the cave, he noticed a huge sword hanging on the wall, a sword that must have belonged to a giant. Beowulf leapt into the air and grabbed it from the wall. The Sea Hag leapt after him. Beowulf swung the mighty blade through the air as the demon attacked.

Her head rolled onto the ground.

Beowulf watched the green blood trickle down the blade. It fizzed and ate away at the metal, dissolving it slowly. He saw Grendel's corpse lying on the ground at the other end of the cave, so with another mighty blow, Beowulf beheaded the Sea Hag's son. The blood of Grendel dissolved the blade completely, leaving only the handle of the weapon in Beowulf's hand.

Tucking the handle into his belt, the

warrior took the heads of both demons in one hand and dived into the water.

The serpents had now gone and Beowulf swam safely to the shore. There, he was met with a huge cheer as he threw the heads of Grendel and the Sea Hag at Hrothgar's feet. Four Danish warriors lifted the heads of the demons onto spears and carried them back to Heorot.

Back in the Great Hall everyone gathered at Beowulf's feet to hear his story, "I praise God that I was victorious! The demons are gone and the land is safe. I must now return to my own kingdom but know that if any other demons threaten the safety of the Danes you will always have the protection of Beowulf!"

Another celebratory feast was held. Beowulf presented the handle of his sword to Unferth as a trophy of his victory. He then gave Hrothgar the handle of the giant's sword he had used to behead the beasts. Dressed in glorious gold the warriors from Geatland went back to the shore where the coastguard had Beowulf's ship made ready.

Hrothgar embraced Beowulf like a son and swore eternal friendship to him and his men.

The rowan tree ship then sailed across the waters to Geatland. There, the warriors marched to Hygelac's Hall, told of their great deeds and presented the treasure that Beowulf had won to Hygelac.

Hygelac threw a feast in Beowulf's honour and presented him with huge tracts of land to the north of the country as well as a mighty sword.

***

Years of peace passed. But in time, a battle between Geats and Shylfings ensued. Hygelac fell in battle and died, so once more mighty Beowulf was sent for, to bring peace to the land.

And he did bring peace. But he did not use his sword to bring this peace. Beowulf's greatest triumph was settled with debate and discussion. Compromises were reached and alliances formed.

Beowulf was crowned King of the Geats. He was a great king, for fifty years his Kingdom of Geatland knew only victories and greatness.

One day the servant of a nearby lord ran away to avoid another beating from his master. As he fled he stumbled and fell. He tripped into an underground cave in which he saw many wonders. There was more gold than anyone could ever imagine! However, the cave smelt of death and darkness.

The servant grabbed a gem studded gold cup and decided to buy his freedom from his master with it. He climbed out of the cave but heard a deafening sound as he did so.

The treasure guarding dragon had been awoken from a thousand winters' long sleep by the thief. He hated being disturbed, so its fury was immense as it stretched its wings and limbs.

The servant ran for his life. Ran as fast as he could. Ran to tell his King what he had seen.

The servant was dragged before Beowulf and he told the warrior of his cowardly act and terrible discovery. News of the dragon's destruction soon spread across the kingdom. The dragon had climbed from its underground den and taken to the skies. It spat venom onto the land. Farms were destroyed, buildings reduced to rubble, warriors killed. Beowulf's own home to the north of the country was destroyed.

Beowulf ordered that a huge all-iron shield be made by the blacksmiths.

Then putting his battle gear on and holding his sword at his side, he chose eleven of his most loyal warriors and set off to find this monstrous enemy.

The servant timidly led the way to the cave. Beowulf and the eleven warriors followed close behind; the thirteen of them rode across Geatland.

The dragon had returned to its underground lair and had gone back to sleep.

Beowulf leapt from his horse and listened to its snores at the cave entrance.

"Come foul beast! Face me! I am Beowulf!!!"

The dragon heard the sound of a human voice disturbing its slumber. It swiftly uncoiled itself, left its heap of gold and burst out of the underground cave with a roar of fury.

Ten of the eleven warriors and the servant thief screamed in terror and ran as fast as they could to the safety of the trees beyond. Only the warrior Wiglaf remained at his King's side.

Wiglaf turned and began to shout at his cowardly comrades for leaving their King.

But Beowulf was not discouraged, he let out a mighty battle cry and charged at the dragon. He swung his sword and hacked at the red scales of the dragon repeatedly, but the blade merely bounced off the rock-like scales.

Flames burst from the dragon's mouth, enveloping Beowulf completely. Only his great shield protected him from the fiery breath. Beowulf staggered back and fell to the ground, the dragon throwing more and more hot flames upon him.

Wiglaf let out his mighty battle cry and charged at the dragon, thrusting his blade at its soft yellow underbelly scales.

The dragon roared in pain. Beowulf, seeing his comrade's bravery, leapt to Wiglaf's side and together they hacked the dragon down. Beowulf threw his heavy shield behind him and used both hands to direct his sword to the dragon's heart.

With its last breath the dragon let out a final burst of fire and Beowulf was consumed by the flames. His burnt body fell backwards onto the charred earth.

Wiglaf jumped to his King's side and tried to tend to his wounds.

"No, dear Wiglaf," whispered Beowulf, "I am done. But before I die I wish to see the treasure that the dragon was guarding. Let me look upon the beauty of it before I die."

So Wiglaf carried the treasure up from the cave and piled high the gold before his King.

Beowulf's face was illuminated by the sight before him and he breathed his last breath.

Wiglaf cried and moaned. The ten warriors who had abandoned Beowulf emerged from the woods and Wiglaf chased them away from his King.

He carried Beowulf's body back to his Great Hall. There, Wiglaf ordered that a huge barrow should be built on the cliffs of the shore so that all would be able to see it from miles around.

Then they built a funeral pyre next to the barrow. Wiglaf set it on fire and the great King of Geatland was burnt in this pyre. The smoke drifted into the Heavens, while the Geats marched around the fire. Beowulf's

ashes were buried in the barrow together with
the dragon's treasure.

The Greatest King on Earth was dead. Death
comes to us all. But his words and deeds
would live on in the stories told of him.
Wiglaf became the new King of Geatland . . .
and he would also be a great king . . .

Also available from:

PUBLISHING

The Kings of Ancient Greece by Adam Bushnell
ISBN 978-1-905637-84-3
King Midas . . . King Sisyphus . . . King Minos . . . These
three kings were the craziest, cleverest and cruellest of all
of the Kings of Ancient Greece. Their stories tell the tales of
Heracles, Pegasus, Icarus, the dreaded Minotaur and many
more famous mythical characters.
Suitable for 9 – 12 year olds.

Snakes' Legs and Cows' Eggs by Adam Bushnell
ISBN 978-1-905637-21-8
Selected for the SLA Boys into Books (5-11) 2008 List.

Donkeys' Wings and Worms' Stings by Adam Bushnell
ISBN 978-1-905637-50-8

Fishes' Claws and Dinosaurs' Paws by Adam Bushnell
ISBN 978-1-905637-76-8
What happens when you sneeze with your eyes open? When
a woodcutter meets a dragon? When a giant wants a new
slave? Or when fire monsters try to keep the world feeling
icy?
The three books above include traditional tales and brand
new stories, each told with serious silliness. Each book
comprises of eight stories which bring together characters
from all over the world.
Suitable for 8 – 12 year olds.

Whispers in the Woods by Mark Bartholomew
ISBN 978-1-904904-61-8
Discovered lost in the woods and taken in by local
villagers, two mysterious green children find themselves
caught up in a quest to track down their missing father.
They encounter many strange and wonderful characters
but none are more terrifying than Silas of Wickham, the
witch finder who relentlessly pursues them to the sea.
Suitable for 9 year olds and above.

Chaos in the Cathedral by Mark Bartholomew
ISBN 978-1-904904-94-6
The quest of the green children continues as they search
the plague-ridden streets of Lincoln, looking for the one
man who can help them find Robin Hood who might be
their father. The children manage to escape the clutches
of the Master of the Lincoln Gilds and leave chaos in their
wake as they flee the quarantined cathedral before it's too
late! However, in Sherwood, one of them is captured . . .
Suitable for 9 year olds and above.

Swords in the Summer by Mark Bartholomew
ISBN 978-1-905637-31-7
Leaving Sherwood Forest and Robin Hood far behind them,
Fern, Hickory and Nathaniel ride west to the ancient
Celtic land of Cornwall. Here they must find the legendary
warrior known as the Green Knight, but Cornwall is in
the midst of war and the children soon find themselves
embroiled in a bitter struggle to defend the realm against
invasion . . .
Suitable for 9 year olds and above.

Beneath the Bombers' Moon by David Webb
ISBN 978-1-900818-33-9
It is October 1940 and the air raids have begun over
Thornley. Sparky and his best friend, John, like to spend
time with Sparky's uncle in the signal box at the train
station. One day they overhear the guards discussing the
two ammunition trains that have been hit, one in Coventry
and the other in Liverpool. The next one will soon be
passing through Thornley . . . will Thornley be a target?
Is information being passed to the Germans? If so, who is
doing it?
Suitable for 8 - 12 year olds.

Eye of the Storm by David Webb
ISBN 978-1-900818-56-8
Danny Sharpe didn't really want to go to the City Museum
in the first place. At the end of the afternoon, Mr Willis,
Danny's teacher, is desperate to get his class back to school
before a thunderstorm breaks out, but Danny has lost his
bag. When Danny wanders into the museum's Victorian
street, the storm breaks with full force, and Danny
embarks on the adventure of a lifetime . . .
Suitable for 8 - 12 year olds.

Bad Influence by Steven Lockyer
ISBN 978-1-904374-34-3
Polly Taylor is an intelligent, thoughtful 10-year-old, who
lives with her mum and moody older brother Chris. She
has an Uncle Jim, who asks her to look after a disk, and to
be careful . . . very careful. What he didn't tell her was that
it was dangerous and could change people's lives. Polly
being intrigued uses the disk and – oh dear, did she see
some changes!!!
Suitable for 9 - 13 year olds.

Watchers of the Sky by Stephanie Baudet
ISBN 978-1-904904-43-4
Since witnessing the plane crash in which Douglas Bader lost his legs, Philip has admired the air ace as he copes with such a disability. He himself suffers from dyslexia and although no name has yet been given to it, he knows that he is not as stupid as everyone thinks. Bader's true exploits are relayed to Philip by his aircraft engineer father. Philip prepares to leave school and hold down a part time job, as well as coping with rationing, air raids and the discovery of a German parachute . . .
Suitable for 9 -14 year olds

Moving On by Margaret Nash
ISBN 978-1-904904-42-7
Moving On is a story that takes place in the late 1950s/early 1960s when motorbikes and pop music were 'the thing'. The story is loosely set in Liverpool amongst newly opened Wimpy bars, Beatles' music, sky scraper buildings and the old pea-souper fogs.
Suitable for 10 -14 year olds

Mrs Wrelton's Dinosaur by Ian MacDonald
ISBN 978-1-904374-48-0
Spike is a large, green, papier-mâché dinosaur. He has been in Mrs Wrelton's classroom for years and has always answered the register! Until, that is, one day the class have a clean up and Spike is seen in the rubbish skip. Sam, Suhail and Amy set off on a dangerous adventure to save Spike . . .
Suitable for 7 - 10 year olds.

Order online @ www.eprint.co.uk